D1585977

The Adventures of

Jack and Adam

WANTED

Anthony Broderick

Copyright © Anthony Broderick, 2016

First Published in Ireland, in 2016, in co-operation with
Choice Publishing, Drogheda, County Louth, Republic of Ireland.
www.choicepublishing.ie

Paperback ISBN: 978-1-911131-10-6

eBook ISBN: 978-1-911131-93-9 The Larry Right Series

All rights reserved. No part of this publication may be reproduced,
stored in a retrieval system, transmitted in any form, or by any means,
electronic, mechanical, photocopying, recording or otherwise, without
the prior permission of the copyright holder.

This book is a work of fiction. All characters in this book are fictitious,
and any resemblance to actual persons, living or dead, is purely
coincidental. Names, characters, places or incidents are a product of
the author's imagination and are used fictitiously.

A CIP catalogue record for this book is available from
the National Library.

Introduction

Welcome to the beginning of a series of intriguing stories following the adventures of two young brothers and their pets, Club and Diamond, along with their family and friends. 'Wanted' introduces you to the brothers, Jack and Adam. Summer holidays are fast approaching, and with the holidays comes a sinister adventure into the strange world of a wayward scientist who inflicts his cruelty upon the most innocent inhabitants of Willows Town.

With a mixture of excitement and humour, Jack and Adam follow a summertime adventure, discovering that not all is as it should be in their neck of the woods.

Chapter 1 – Crumbs

"I'm in here!" shouted Jack, almost falling off the toilet seat in fright.

"Sorry, sorry!" Adam replied, as he quickly closed the bathroom door and made his way to the kitchen.

"Why doesn't he lock the door when he's going to the toilet?" asked Adam, calling to his mother who was eating a sandwich.

"Give him a few minutes and he will be out, or else use the toilet upstairs," she mumbled.

Just then they heard the flushing sound and the tap being turned on. Jack marched out and immediately asked if there was any food for him.

Jack was Adam's brother and was always involved in devilment. Even at the age of three, when he jumped down on the end of a seesaw in playschool, just to see their neighbour Bobby, who was small for his age, go flying up into the air and land straight down on his head, Mum knew he was going to be a tough one.

Adam and Jack were in fourth class in a boys' primary school. Adam had stayed back a year and as a result the two of them were now in the same class. Adam was gentler and shyer than Jack. He regularly read books at home and did his homework for at least an hour after school. He was quite clever in some subjects but overall needed to get regular help from resource teachers, especially in the area of maths. This held him back at school. His brother never tried hard in his school work but always seemed to get all the answers correct and could think of great questions to ask the teacher.

Jack was much more popular with his classmates, as he was constantly annoying teachers and would do anything for a laugh. Amazingly, however, the teachers could never really fault him in terms of his academic ability, and he was once described in a report card as being "sometimes the best and the worst pupil to have in a classroom". Adam never liked it when the teachers said to Jack, "If only you were more like your brother." Adam was nearly two years older than his brother, so he really felt out of place being in fourth class with him.

At home life was quite different. Jack and Adam got on very well together and really enjoyed venturing into the garden and exploring the surrounding area with their partners, Club and Diamond.

Club was a medium-sized white Labrador who had been well trained and loved ever since she was a puppy. She seemed to be ever ready to play and follow you continuously. At night she was a very good watch dog and defended the property with her distinctive growl and bark. The hair on her back sometimes turned golden when she was in an attacking mode.

Diamond was quite the opposite. She was a small, greyish black cat with a white stripe on her tail. A burglar could be breaking in through a back window and she would just purr up against him and lie down for a massage. She was inclined to stare in through the window with what seemed to be a dirty cunning look, but could easily be partial blindness.

What was incredible was how well these two animals got on in each other's company. They spent the day while the boys were at school curled against one another. At ten past three, when Jack and Adam arrived home from school, the two of them were always lined up at the door, waiting for their regular feed of nuts and cat food.

Jack and Adam had a large area of garden at the back of their yellow-painted house. There was lots of space, plenty of trees to climb and bushes to crawl under. Jack had helped his Dad build a large treehouse at the end of the garden, and that was where the boys discussed their next plan of attack. The treehouse was built on top of four oak tree trunks. It had high steps leading up to the door with two small windows. Club and Diamond made themselves at home in the area, so when it was raining they had a nice little shelter to stay in.

"Oh no – look who it is again!" shrieked Jack when he saw Mr Dot making his way over from next door.

"What's wrong this time, did Club do her business in his garden?" asked Adam. He smirked from ear to ear and looked around to see if Club was nearby.

"Come on, let's check it out!" called Jack, racing down the treehouse steps.

At the front door Mr Dot's voice was heard complaining that Club had left a mess on his back lawn again.

"It's not good enough, and you're making too much of a racket with all those drills. Ralf is trying to study for his exams and he cannot concentrate with all this commotion!" shouted Mr Dot, and spit flew out the sides of his mouth.

"I'll take care of it," said Jack, walking into his house to grab a plastic bag and perform the hateful task of removing Club's droppings from Mr Dot's back lawn.

Dad scratched his head and nodded as Mr Dot stormed off back to his house.

"Come on, the boys will take care of that. Don't let him ruin your day," said Mum, patting her husband on the shoulder to calm his nerves.

Jack threw Club a slight smile as he wrapped the plastic bag around the droppings, holding his breath. "Right, what will we do for the day?" he shouted to Adam, firing the plastic bag into a bin before jumping the wall back to the treehouse.

"*The Larry Right Hour* is on TV at twelve o'clock, so for the next while I think we should try and sneak into Granny's house and grab a few biscuits before it starts," Adam replied, eyeing up the area on the opposite side of the Dots.

The Larry Right Hour was a cartoon that the boys tried not to miss. They felt it was an important part of their life's education. Larry, the main character, was a young boy who could turn any situation into profit. He had the contacts and know-how to create empires from seemingly ordinary ideas. It was always nice to have something sweet to chew on while enjoying one of Larry's ingenious schemes.

Mum only allowed the boys to have one or two biscuits each day and maybe a little surprise on a Friday, if they were good. However, Adam and Jack had back-up plans. They knew that during the day their Granny normally left her door unlocked and kept the biscuit tin about two yards from the entrance. This was a little mission that they undertook regularly and so far they had never got caught.

Granny was getting quite old and had been living on her own since her husband died five years ago. She enjoyed cooking for the family each week and some of the desserts they got from her would make your mouth water. The highlight of every Sunday afternoon was when Granny threw a little stone against the window. This signalled that the dessert was ready. The boys were very lucky to be living beside her as she often minded them when their parents were out, and she spoiled them rotten.

"Right, we'll head for Base One," Adam announced. He reached for the treehouse door and began sneaking down the wooden steps, getting into character as an escaped convict.

Jack followed closely behind, with Club and Diamond scampering along for fear they would miss out on something. Adam led the way to the back of the shed. He jumped the wall and Jack soon followed suit.

The wall was high, but the boys were very fit, so no climb really fazed them. They knew that the best route to get inside and grab the biscuits without being spotted was around the back of Granny's house.

"Ouch!" Jack cried as a nettle grazed his shin.

"Be careful of that barbed wire!" Adam hissed as he carefully ducked underneath it.

They had to make their way through a small patch of land where cattle grazed and often charged up and down the field.

Jack flinched for a moment as he saw the bullock resting in the middle of the field, with its two cut horns on its intimidating head. Previously Jack had had an unpleasant experience with this bullock when he was trying to fetch a ball that had landed beside it. The bullock had charged at him and if it hadn't been for Jack's swift movement, he might have been knocked down. Adam turned back and could see the fear in his brother.

"Come on, he has his back turned," shouted Adam, trying to encourage Jack to put the past behind him.

Jack broke a medium-sized stick off a nearby tree and held it tightly in his fist.

"If it tries to charge at me this time, I'll threaten him with this," he said, smacking the stick against the barbed wire.

The brothers could hear Club moaning as she could not climb over the high wall. Diamond could easily have sprung up on top of it but chose to wait on the nearside.

They knew that if Club was over in Granny's garden there was more chance of them being seen, so it was best to leave her behind.

"Base One" was the code name given to the area behind a large rock in the middle of Granny's garden. They had named it this as it was the first and best place to eye up the window to see if Granny was in the kitchen. Once they had arrived here unseen all they had to do was sneak in, grab from the biscuit tin and race out to behind the rock again. It sounded simple but the plan had to be carried out with precision.

Jack squeezed through the fence, then both boys sprinted over, keeping their heads down and lay tightly behind the large boulder. Adam peered out and reached for his binoculars. He lined the sights up with the window and could see nobody in the kitchen.

"These binoculars are *brilliant*! I can even zoom in on them!" he said with a large grin on his face. "I'll stay here and keep look out, you go and get the goods," he added.

"You make sure you signal me if she comes into sight," replied Jack, realising that he had drawn the short straw this time.

Jack stayed low and raced towards a small bush and then quickly up beside the door. He looked back at Adam to make sure the coast was still clear, and after getting a wave of his hand as the signal, he slowly eased the door open. Although Jack had done this about a hundred times before, he still felt nervous of being caught. After all, he was the one breaking and entering, and who was to say whether Adam wouldn't leg it at any sign of trouble and deny any involvement in this act.

Neither of the boys really wanted to steal from their Granny. It was just the thrill of the "mission" that they enjoyed. After all, Granny would probably give them a whole box of sweets and biscuits if they just asked her.

As the door moved inwards, Jack could hear the television from the next room. It was the familiar sound of Granny's TV show, one which she adored and watched religiously. Jack and Adam sometimes joined her as she watched Monica, the TV character, stick her nose in another problem which didn't concern her and yet again make life miserable for the bad guys. They would try and guess the culprits at the beginning, before the mysterious murders took place. Granny had a good eye for the murderers. "Monica has a shrewd eye," she observed, carefully weighing up each character introduced throughout the investigation.

Jack let out a sigh of relief, as he knew that if the television was on Granny was more than likely sitting down in her big comfortable chair.

He composed himself for a moment and then dragged his knees along the ground until he was right under the biscuit tin. He lifted himself up and quietly opened the shiny silver lid. He was in Adam's sight at this point, and Adam began giggling nervously behind the rock.

Jack could now see the range of biscuits in the container and had to decide what type to grab. There was an abundance to choose from, from jaffa cakes to custard creams. Jack knew that he should never take the last of any biscuit packet but choose a few from an open packet, so it looked like none had been taken. As much as he wanted to grab the delicious-looking twin pack of jaffa cakes, they were not open, so he could not take them. There were some custard creams and digestives lying in the tin and they would never be missed, he thought. He filled his hands with them and then reached for the lid to place it back on, accidentally dropping some crumbs onto the ground.

He suddenly heard the volume on the TV being lowered, and knew that this meant that Granny had heard something. She would either go to the toilet or the kitchen. Either way, he had to make a very swift exit. He maintained his low centre of gravity and hurried to the door, which he had left ajar. He pulled himself out and, as quietly as he could, began to close the door behind him.

Just as he was closing it, a digestive biscuit fell to the ground. He stopped for a second and thought about going back for it. In the distance he could see Adam frantically making the signal over and over.

Judging by the panic on Adam's face, Jack understood he had to get out of there ASAP. He lowered his back to keep out of sight from window level and ran as fast as a hare back to

Adam behind the rock, leaving a trail of biscuits after him. He dived to the ground like a soldier going into the trenches to take cover.

"Did she see us?" Jack asked, panting just like Club after a chase.

"What took you so long? That was a close one!" cried Adam, smirking at the state his brother was in.

The biscuits in Jack's hands had now disintegrated into dust, and with the sweat running down his palms they looked anything but appetising. Adam peered into his binoculars and focused on the kitchen again. Granny was now in there and seemed to be looking around at the biscuit tin, slightly baffled.

"We'd better get back to the treehouse before she sees us here," said Adam. "As soon as she leaves the kitchen, we'll run for it," he added.

The two boys got ready and soon raced over to the fence, through the patch of land, and back over the wall to their own property. Club was the first one to greet Jack as he hopped down onto the uncut grass.

"Get off!" shouted Jack, as Club tried her best to get some of the broken biscuits in his hand.

"Well that was a bit of a disaster," sighed Adam.

He and his brother made their way up the lawn and into the house just in time for *The Larry Right Hour*.

Chapter 2 – Morning Maths

The weekend flew by and Adam and Jack were soon going through the usual routine on a Sunday evening before going to bed. Mum generally spent the evening ironing their school uniforms for the week ahead, while Dad would either be giving out about pairs of socks not matching or ordering some buns for his lunch at work on Monday.

Adam got that anxious knot in his stomach about this time, just as he was getting his bags packed and looking over some of the homework from the weekend. He really disliked going to school. A lot of the material was confusing for him, and he felt a bit different from the others because he had to spend a lot of his time going to remedial classes or getting special help from separate teachers.

Jack, on the other hand, flew around the house with his new cowboy gun loaded with caps. He didn't have a care in the world and the thought of going to school for another week never fazed him. He was never bothered if he hadn't finished some of his lessons, as getting into trouble was just another day at the office. It must be a great feeling, Adam thought, knowing how to do more or less everything in the school books, as he watched Jack aiming his plastic gun high to shoot down several birds from the kitchen window.

"Pack your bags and leave them at the door," said Mum, trying to get the school preparations all complete before she gathered her thoughts for her own work in the morning.

Ordinarily the boys watched some telly just before bedtime and then it was lights out. They were very fortunate as they had a large sitting room for relaxing and watching their favourite programmes. Adam normally did his study and homework upstairs in his room, while Jack preferred to do a little here and a little there, often venturing from kitchen to bedroom – even to the bathroom – carrying his maths copy and book with him.

As Adam went to bed that night he dreamt of the fast approaching summer holidays and all the fun that he and Jack were going to have during this time. Two months of no school was like winning the lotto to Adam. He pulled the sheets up over himself and nestled his head into his soft pillow.

The trip to school was relatively short for the two brothers. They often cycled, but these days they were fortunate enough that Mum was starting work at the same time as school, so she drove them. After feeding Club and Diamond separately, they hopped into the car and off they went.

The school was situated right in the centre of Willows Town, their local town. Willows Town was so called as it was a town designed to absorb the population of the surrounding areas, just like the roots of a willow tree absorbing water. It was an expanding town thanks to the influx of people from Beach Heaven, the nearest city. Most people knew each other and would stop and chat on the street.

There were two little shops, one at either end of the town, where everyone could get their groceries and other items they needed. The one at the bottom of the town was owned by a retired couple known as Mr and Mrs Pegs, and the one at the top of the town, which was the more popular, was run by a man called Mr Hartigan. Mr Hartigan attracted the most customers, as his shop was located right beside the church. After mass everyone popped in to get their weekly shopping before heading back to their homes.

There was one bank and one post office that offered employment to lots of families. There were three pubs, but most people went to the same one, The Willows Inn, every weekend – and some went daily. On a Saturday night, music could be heard in all directions, filtering down alleyways and laneways. The boys had only been in it once for their cousin's confirmation, but looked forward to the day when they could enjoy the music and dance with their friends.

There was also a butcher's shop just up from The Willows Inn run by a woman called Mrs

Slate. She sold the freshest meat in all of Willows Town. Children loved accompanying their parents into Mrs Slate's, as she offered them free lollipops and sometimes chocolate.

As the boys passed by the swimming pool their eyes lit up, hoping Mum would bring them there at the weekend.

"The swimming pool showers are so nice," said Jack, reflecting on the twenty or so minutes he had spent in them last week.

"Yes, and going to the shop after a swim is essential to restore all that lost energy," replied Adam, winking at his brother. He was trying to hint to his Mum that she should bring them to the shop for some sweets every time they finished a swim.

On the way to school they frequently kept an eye out for a man known as 'The Wanderer'. He was a stranger in one sense, but everyone knew who he was, wandering up and down the town each day, hoping that people would give him money to buy some food. Not much was known about this character but he was believed to have been an old soldier who had fought in the war.

How he ended up with no money was a mystery.

The boys could also spot him by his dark tanned skin and the limp in his left leg, presumably the result of war. Sometimes he struggled to get to his feet after spending time sitting on the main street. Jack and Adam were fascinated at the way he would look so pathetic when approaching people.

"No, he is not around today. Maybe he found some shelter last night and is having a lie in!" said Jack sarcastically. Mum did not really want to laugh but could not help releasing a little smirk from the corner of her mouth.

When they got back to school on a Monday morning the boys always enjoyed chatting to their classmates about the antics they had got up to over the weekend. For Adam this was the calm before the storm, as he relaxed with his friends and waited for the class teacher, Mr Atkinson, to drive up in his Perkin.

The Perkin was a new design of car that had just been released. It was very square and looked an awkward vehicle to drive and park. Mr Atkinson's Perkin was mustard yellow in colour and had a big tow hitch on the back. Jack joked about this car to his classmates and always wondered why Mr Atkinson just did not buy a nicer car, like a Claxon X11, with all the money he was earning.

When the children saw him stepping out of the car at exactly seven minutes past nine, as he did each morning, they let out a sigh of disappointment.

"Damn it!" cried Jack. "Pity that sub, Mr Henderson, isn't teaching us today. He's very nice."

"It's a shame he can't teach us all the time instead of this—"

"He's coming!" the fourth class boys called out, and everyone raced back to their desks and sat up straight.

Mr Atkinson walked in wearing his well-ironed white shirt. He usually wore one of three colours of shirt: pink, blue or white. It was just a theory, but some boys in the class noticed that when he wore a pink shirt he was much more cross than other days. However, when he wore the white shirt his mood seemed to be more tolerable and he did not seem to pick on individuals in the class as much. The blue shirt was only worn on rare occasions and nobody had yet figured out what it meant.

"Good morning, class!" said Mr Atkinson in a chirpy manner.

"Good morning, sir," each pupil in the class responded unenthusiastically.

"I hope all homework is complete and everyone is ready for some lessons today – isn't that right, Jack?"

"Yes, sir, all homework complete!" Jack proudly replied to the teacher.

Each pupil in the class forced back a laugh, as they knew quite well that Jack had probably only finished a small part of his weekend homework.

"Take out your maths homework and maths books!" Mr Atkinson ordered.

The class reluctantly reached for their school bags and placed their open copies onto the table for correction.

Adam had a worried look on his face and his cheeks had gone slightly pale. He just wanted maths to be out of the way. Adam sat beside his friend Paul.

Paul was probably the best in the class at maths, and each time they were given work to complete, Paul confidently flew through the sums, while Adam attempted one sum over and over again. There were pros and cons to sitting beside a student like Paul. On the one hand, it was great for Adam to get much needed help with some of the work, but on the other hand, his presence made Adam feel more and more inferior.

Mr Atkinson favoured the people who were good at maths, as that was his favourite subject to teach. Those that lagged behind at this subject were often shouted at and occasionally humiliated in front of the class. Adam found that Mr Atkinson never taught maths very well, as he presumed that everyone knew how to do it already. At home his Dad often went through parts of a sum, starting with the basics and encouraging him to do his best. Adam found he worked better in this environment as he wasn't placed under the same pressure as in the classroom.

At half nine he heard a familiar knock on the classroom door. It was Miss Harold, who sometimes took him out during maths to give him one-to-one help. Mr Atkinson threw a sharp look over at Adam, reminding him that he was unlike the other boys because he struggled at maths. Jack never liked how this teacher picked on Adam, and that was probably one of the main reasons he often caused trouble in class.

Adam grabbed his folder and followed Miss Harold down the long corridor to a small room across from one of the emergency exits.

"How was your weekend?" Miss Harold started off by asking, as she tidied her messy desk for her day's work.

"Good, thanks!" Adam replied briskly, not wanting to get into a conversation about it.

He started looking at his worksheets, but ducked down when he heard older boys carrying messages for their class teachers. Miss Harold could sense his embarrassment, so she closed the door to prevent any strays wandering in for a look.

The lunchtime bell brought a roar of satisfaction throughout the school. The boys rarely spent any time eating their lunch. They would just grab a ball from the classroom and take a brisk walk out of the big doors to the yard. Most of the pupils in fourth class played football during the two breaks, although some preferred to spend the time chatting or playing other games like "catch" or "tip the can". There was a vast play area in the school yard. Each class had their designated space, but the sixth class were envied, as they had control of the big pitch.

Mr Donald, the principal, spent every Monday lunchtime on yard duty. He was a nice old man who regularly gave them a few minutes extra to play if the weather was fine. He was coming up to retirement and was beginning to ease off, so he tried not to get too wound up at silly incidents. Some pupils tried to take advantage of this, but the majority respected him for all the work he had done in and around the school and showed him the special regard he deserved.

The last few weeks of term gradually passed and the holidays were approaching. The summer exams were now the biggest focus for Adam as he certainly had to improve on last year's score. He put in a big effort each evening and really focused on getting a better grade, especially in maths. Jack, on the other hand, was mainly trying to improve his classroom behaviour. His previous report card had resulted in him having to stay in and do dishes for one solid week.

"I cannot be spending my time washing and drying dishes this summer!" said Jack to Adam anxiously.

"Just be a little less hyper in class and focus on staying in your seat," his brother replied, knowing well that was harder than it sounded for a young boy who was as fidgety as a hamster.

Adam advised Jack to buy Mr Atkinson a little present on the last day of school, just to get on his good side.

"I should buy him a can of spray paint for his car!" Jack laughed. He reached into his drawer to find some loose change.

Jack ended up buying Mr Atkinson a little candle and a card. "Hopefully it will do the trick," he giggled as he wrapped the candle in colourful paper, trusting that Mr Atkinson would appreciate it.

Chapter 3 – The Raft of Discovery

After the last school day had finally come to an end, the boys excitedly hopped on the bus at ten past three. Jack and Adam were on a high. The day had taken so long to arrive, especially for Adam, but thankfully he had gotten successfully through fourth class. Jack had ended up on a good note with Mr Atkinson and he felt confident about his report card, which was due to be posted next week.

Each pupil on board the bus was ecstatic with the thought of no school for the next two months. The weather was forecast to be fine for July, which was an added bonus.

When the bus stopped at their house, Adam and Jack jumped off and greeted Club with a big hug. Club growled in anticipation of her container of nuts. Her nose was wet as it brushed against Adam's cheerful face. Her hair had been shedding for the last month, which meant your clothes would be destroyed if she jumped up on you. Adam reached first for the tin of cat food and scraped the last remaining scoop out for Diamond, who had perched herself on top of the recycling bin to await her afternoon meal. The two pets always put everyone in a good mood, it did not matter what else was going on in life. Rubbing and cuddling the two of them was a remedy for stress.

Jasmine, the brothers' minder for the past few years, greeted the two as they came in like happy ducklings. She had some hot soup poured out in matching bowls, with a couple of fresh, crunchy rolls.

"It's great to be off," Jack explained to Jasmine. "It's almost like we have been let free for the next two months."

"I know, it's great," Jasmine responded gently, pouring out some lemonade and ice from the cold jug.

Jasmine was on her holidays also. She had spent the last year living in the city where she had just completed her first year of training to be a music teacher. Music was her passion and when she did not have the radio on in the kitchen, the boys often saw her tossing her long black hair to songs she hummed in her head. Diamond would sit up on the window ledge any time Jasmine played her accordion, and doze. It would be great if you could hypnotise her, Jack often thought, watching this creature fall deeper and deeper into meditation.

"Well done anyway, boys. You two are moving on quickly now – going into fifth class next term," said Jasmine, leaning up against one of the presses. "How are you going to spend the long summer ahead?" she asked, smiling from ear to ear.

Adam and Jack glanced at each other, knowing that there would not be a day over the summer when they would be stuck for something to do.

The boys thoroughly enjoyed having Jasmine in the house as she was not very strict and often left them alone to do what they wanted. She was a good cook and normally gave their parents good reports about their conduct at the end of the day. Adam and Jack often played practical jokes on Jasmine, just for a little bit of fun.

One time they went a little too far. The two had often wondered what weight she was so they came up with a plan to find out. They left a weighing scale outside the bathroom door, with a little white sheet covering it. Jack hid under a pile of clothes next to the scale and waited there to see what number popped up on the screen when she stepped on it. Unfortunately she ended up stepping on the glass part of the scale and broke it completely. They felt bad after doing this, but soon got over it when they received water guns as birthday presents. They started off spraying each other, but soon focused their attacks on moving cars and the odd pedestrian passing by the front of the house.

That evening Dad reached for his keys and headed towards the garden shed. It was time to give the lawn a cut and that was Dad's favourite weekly chore. He owned a ride-on lawnmower and he was in his element spinning around, taking pride in the cut.

"♪ La dee dee la dee da ♫" Dad chirped as he pinned back the metal door of the shed so the lawnmower could fit out.

Adam made his way over to the lawnmower and pulled off the covering sheets that protected it against bird droppings. Club suddenly took off at a fast gallop, up to the top of the huge pile of turf from last year at the back of the shed.

"Oh no, she's gone up on top again!" Jack said.

Club had no fear of climbing up any height, but it was in coming down that she faced her biggest challenge. She got a little scared and the boys either had to pull her down with their hands or lure her back with some food.

"She must have seen a mouse or something. Try and get her down before she causes an avalanche of turf!" said Dad. He pointed towards the top pile.

Jack was the first to climb up on the turf heap, and he found himself staring into a blinding swarm of turf mould.

"Oh the dust!" Adam cried out, waving his hand to waft away the debris. The boys could see that Club had followed something into a gap in the blockwork. She was sniffing around with her tail wagging vigorously.

"Come on, Club, let's go back down!" moaned Jack. He mounted the highest pile of turf and leant forward to investigate.

It was very humid up this high in the turf shed and getting more difficult to breathe. Jack turned his head to the side, coughing in the thick dust. As he did so, something interesting caught his eye. Further back, hidden beneath a large pile of loose turf, Jack could see some type of handle. It looked like a handle of a bike or even part of a go-cart. It was red in colour and was attached to something.

"What's that?" Jack shouted as he pointed in the direction of the strange object.

Adam carefully pulled himself closer, trying to keep his balance.

"I don't know, let's check it out," he said.

The two boys, ignoring Club for now, ventured over to explore. Jack was the first on the scene and quickly began pulling up turf around the red object to find out what exactly was being covered.

Adam helped in the clearing process and gradually they revealed a large pallet with two blue barrels attached. The red object that they had thought was a handle now appeared to be a type of lever. It was attached to the wooden pallet.

The brothers looked at each other in astonishment. Dad, who had noticed turf flying in every direction, now looked up and asked what Adam and Jack were doing.

"We have found something here, Dad. It looks like a raft of some sort!" Adam called out, excitement in his voice.

Dad took one big step up on top of a large stack of turf so that he could see what the boys were rummaging at. He was interested now, and a little baffled, so he made his way up to where the boys were kneeling. There was so much dust that he had to cough several times to clear his throat.

"The old raft!" he cried in amazement. "*This* is where it was for all of those years!"

He knelt down to get a closer look, placing his hand on the red lever like it was bringing back memories. Dad told them that this raft was one he had made years ago for travelling down the stream with an old friend. He began touching the barrels and sides of the raft, shocked that it was in such good shape after all this time.

"Will it still work?" Jack asked, trying to pull it free.

Dad and Adam helped remove the last few sods of turf and heaved and heaved until it was brought up to the surface. Adam and Jack both made their way down to the ground as Dad lowered the old raft along the side. The boys helped place it on the ground and turned it upright.

Dad caught hold of Club, who was now as black as soot from rolling around in the turf mould, and brought her towards the ground with him. The boys helped their father drag the raft out to the middle of the shed for further inspection. They could see that the pallet needed some repair and one of the barrels had a large dent in its side.

"Did this really work?" Adam asked his Dad. "Could you actually sit on it and go down the stream?"

"Oh yes, it really did," Dad replied. "When I was your age, my friend and I brought it down to the woods and we would sail down the stream for hours."

"Wow, cool!" Jack responded, looking at the raft with eager anticipation. "Can we fix it up and have a go ourselves?"

"Sure we'll do even better," answered Dad. "We'll build a new and improved raft made of new material. We'll just leave this to the side for the time being and tomorrow after work we'll start our new project."

"Brilliant!" shouted the boys simultaneously, punching the air with delight.

Even Club knew there was something exciting happening and she raced around the shed, head down, like a mad hare.

During the next few days the brothers looked forward to going down to the shed after Dad had finished work, to begin making the different parts of the new raft. Dad was a very skilled carpenter and both Jack and Adam knew that this was going to be a product of high quality. Dad had organised a new wooden pallet and two new barrels to make it float. Jack, who was quite a good painter, helped apply a type of varnish to the surface which prevented the water from seeping through and damaging the timber. Adam handed his Dad screw after screw as the raft was made more sturdy and durable.

Dad explained to his sons that the red lever was used as a steering wheel. It was a long piece of timber at the back of the raft, connected to an oar underneath, which guided the raft down the stream. There was a red handle placed over the piece of timber again to prevent water from rotting it. Dad told the two boys that if you wanted to steer to the left you pulled the handle to the right, and vice versa.

Like his brother, Adam enjoyed doing a little art at school, and painted several designs on the two blue barrels just to make them colourful. Once everything was complete Jack was eager to find a stream to put the raft to the test.

"Where did you say the stream was?" asked Jack, looking up eagerly at his father as he applied the finishing touches to the timber.

"There is a long stream down in the woods that I will bring you two to see and try this raft out on during the weekend," Dad answered. "It's getting too late now and your mother has some tea ready for us in the house," he added.

"I'm looking forward to that!" said Adam. He lifted himself up and stood back to admire the designs he had created.

The boys finished packing away the extra screws and helped shut the two large shed doors.

Before Jack went to sleep that night he imagined what it would be like to float down the stream on this new raft. He tossed and turned with anticipation as he waited for morning to arrive.

Chapter 4 – The Woodsman

The morning sun brought a ray of light to Jack's top window. He jumped out of his bed and immediately looked around for the old rough clothes he wore for messing about outside during the summer. He grabbed his light blue jumper covered in bits of dry paint. He loved wearing this jumper, as it gave the impression that he was doing some hard work. As he passed the kitchen window, he noticed that his Dad had already left for work. Mum was inside preparing her lunch.

"Sit down and have a nice bowl of cereal, Jack, before you go outside!" she said, scampering about in her usual panic.

Jack nodded and soon Adam walked into the kitchen to have his bite to eat. The boys then heard the familiar two gentle knocks on the front door.

"That must be Jasmine," said Mum. "Make sure

the two of you are well behaved today for her. Your Dad has told me that he is going to bring you down to the woods to try out the new raft on Saturday, so you can look forward to that!"

Then she opened the front door.

"Good morning!" said Jasmine, entering the kitchen and hanging up her black cardigan on the hook beside the door.

"Hi!" Adam and Jack replied, mouths full, gulping down their cereal.

Within minutes Jack was up from the table, milk dripping down the sides of his mouth. He made his way outside and was soon leapt upon by Club. Adam followed suit and put on his green wellingtons. Diamond had chosen to relax in the shade for the morning and she lay stretched out like a Persian prince.

"All she needs now is someone to feed her some grapes," chuckled Adam as he passed her by.

They met up in the treehouse to begin discussing the various things they would get up to during the day. At the top of the steps the boys noticed that Mr Dot was preparing to mow his lawn. He had cleared all the deckchairs from the grass and was now tugging heavily on the pull-start. By the looks of things he was having some problems starting the engine and appeared to be in a state of frustration.

"I think we should climb up into the trees and throw stones down on the grass before he cuts it," said Jack in a devilish voice.

"We can't do that, Jack," Adam replied quickly. "Remember what happened the last time we tried to pull a stunt on Mr Dot?"

Jack cringed for a moment, remembering the horrible experience of Mr Dot yelling in his face, with spit flying in every direction.

"Ya, you're probably right," Jack answered. He turned back to the treehouse to think of something else to do.

"Why don't we try out the raft down the woods?" he mumbled, not knowing how Adam would react to this idea.

"Dad is bringing us down tomorrow, we have to wait until then," responded Adam, breaking off a twig from the tree.

"But why don't we go down into the woods to see what the stream is like?" Jack said eagerly. "We can drag the raft down. We can just go down for a quick look and be back before

Jasmine even notices that we are gone," he continued.

Adam hesitated for a few moments, wondering whether this was a good idea or not. His instinct told him to stay put, but his sense of adventure was prompting him to take the trip down for a quick look.

"Well, if we just go for a brief walk, just to see how far down it is or how deep the water is," Adam replied in an uncertain manner.

Before he had finished speaking, Jack raced up to the boiler house to get the spare key of the shed and his wellingtons for the trip down the fields.

There was now a spring in Jack's step and Club had picked up the mood, darting from one bush to the other. The boys waved in at Jasmine through the kitchen window just to show her that they were playing safely outside and then hurried down to fetch the raft.

They wanted Club to join them in the woods so they opened a side gate to allow her to enter the first field. Club sometimes drove the cattle in the field mad with her barking and the speed at which she ran. To prevent this, Adam took hold of her collar until both boys had crossed the first gate, into the adjoining field. Thankfully they got safely past the dreaded bullock, who appeared to recognise Jack's blue jumper as he passed.

In the second field the grass was very short and the ground was rather uneven. It was difficult dragging the raft, but thankfully none of the bumps in the land caused any damage. There was a hill leading to the woods that they sometimes slid down during times of snow or ice. The scenery was amazing in this part of the field. All you could see was various green shades of trees and grass stretching for miles. Club was enjoying herself, sniffing at various holes and banks in the earth and occasionally going to the toilet up against a tree.

Adam led the way to a gap in the ditch which they had climbed over before to get down to the woods. It was a relatively easy spot to locate as it was right beside one of the largest oak trees ever seen. The oak tree had been there for as long as the boys or their Dad could remember and had been used for shooting practice by their grandfather when he was alive.

"Mind your step!" Adam called as he climbed carefully over the electric fence.

There were three lines of wire in the fence so it was impossible for the dog to go underneath without getting a shock. They had to lift Club up over the fence and down onto the woodland floor on the other side. Jack caught her and raised her up into Adam's arms.

"Oh the hairs!" Adam cried as he lowered Club onto the pile of leaves, carefully keeping her clear of the electric wire.

Club flicked her legs away from Adam's arms and immediately darted off to explore the nearby area. Adam then took the raft off Jack, tugged it across the wires and lowered it down to the uneven ground.

The two had now arrived at the woods. There were so many trees that the sky was almost blocked out.

"I think these are oak trees, Adam, they're pretty tall!" panted Jack, a little out of breath from lifting both Club and the raft.

Some beams of light shone through branches up high, but most of the area where the boys stood was enclosed by trees. It seemed more like night than day. Adam held a stick in his hand so he could knock away little bits of tree and twigs in his way. Up ahead was a path that stretched away in two directions.

"Which way should we go?" asked Jack, clearing a large cobweb from his face.

"I'm not sure," replied Adam. "I think we might chance walking up to the right," he said hesitantly.

As they walked they could hear a whole range of sounds coming from different parts of the woods. Each bird had its own unique call, and judging by the number of holes in the sides of banks, this was the home to several woodland creatures like foxes, rabbits and squirrels. Club kept running out of sight so Adam had to whistle and call out her name to keep her with them. Like tourists visiting a new city, the brothers walked slowly down the path. They took turns to pull the raft, manoeuvring their way around obstacles, and gazing around at the unfamiliar scenery. Then they heard the trickling of water.

"The stream must be down here!" yelled Jack.

Adam picked up the pace, and sure enough they had found the stream that Dad had told them about. It was a beautifully clean stretch of water that seemed to have a gentle current.

"Wow! The raft will be great on this!" exclaimed Jack.

Adam nodded, and dipped a wellington carefully into the water.

"It's pretty deep!" he said in a surprised tone. "I wonder will the raft support the two of us on it together?"

"There's only one way to find out," answered his brother, easing the raft down the bank and into the water. He steadied it gently with his hands. He crouched down and placed his left leg on the raft, then steadied his body and lifted his right leg on. He reached out to grab some tall plants near the bank, trying his best to hold the raft firm and steady.

"Come on, hop on now," said Jack to his brother.

Adam grabbed Club and guided her down onto the pallet. It didn't really matter if she fell out. She was a decent swimmer and her thick fur acted as a wet suit in the cold.

"Come on! Quickly, Adam!" cried Jack as the raft began to ease away from the bank. Adam, leading with his right leg, leapt next to Club. They were all on board.

Jack decided to man the lever, keeping it central to allow the raft to go straight down the stream with the flow of the water. Adam paddled to give the raft some forward momentum.

"Something isn't right, there is too much weight. It will be better if one of us and Club get off," said Jack, insinuating that he be the one left on board.

Adam realised that Jack was probably right. He stood up and reached for an overhanging branch to pull the raft in.

On the bank, as Adam stood back to think about the situation, he noticed Club perk up her white head. The hair stood up on the back of her head. He stood still, listening to a noise in the distance. It was the sound of someone walking and it seemed to be coming closer and closer.

"Hurry up, grab Club and hide!" hissed Adam. He pulled his wellington out of the soft bank and took cover under a bushy green plant.

Jack quickly hopped off the raft, pulled it close to the bank and took cover. He clutched Club her by her waist and ducked down out of sight.

"Shush!" Jack whispered to Club, praying that she would not bark or make a sound.

Adam, who was nearby, could see the distress Jack was in, trying to keep the dog silent. It wasn't easy, as every last inch of her longed to investigate who this was and bark out loud.

As the sound of footsteps drew close, both boys could see a large male figure wearing a pair of old jeans and a grey woollen jumper. A swarm of flies followed him down the path. He looked about fifty years old and had a very stern look on his face. He had a large stick in one hand which he was swishing back and forth in an effort to get some of the insects off him. From his other hand something was dangling which looked like it was distracting the flies.

Club's mouth started to foam, and Jack gripped her tightly in his right arm. Adam felt very frightened as the grim-faced man passed just a metre above them on the path.

"Please don't see us! Please don't see us!" Adam prayed under his breath.

Club squeezed her head forward, trying to release herself from Jack's tight grip. Her nose sniffed the air, picking up new scents and smells nearby. She let out a little moan in her discomfort.

The man came to an abrupt stop and turned round to see what the noise was.

"Oh no! We will definitely be found now. What are we going to do?" thought Adam anxiously. He bent his head right down.

Jack was in a similar state of panic, his face scrunched up with fear. His instinct was telling him that something about this man didn't look right. He hoped he wouldn't find out what.

The man turned, revealing his rough face, and walked towards the bank of the stream to take a closer look. His eyes looked like something you might see in a Halloween mask. A swarm of midges crowded on his mop of grey, greasy hair.

He shouted something in frustration, waving his stick back and forth. Whatever he said, the boys knew that it wasn't in English.

Then he turned back onto the path and kept walking down through the woods.

Adam waited for a few seconds before letting out a sigh of relief. Jack stayed down until the man had safely moved off along the woodland path, still keeping a firm grip on Club's collar.

"That was too close for comfort!" Jack said, drops of sweat running down his forehead. The brothers composed themselves, waiting for their racing hearts to beat normally once again.

Club had even more froth oozing out of her mouth at this stage and was very pleased to be let free. She headed straight for the stream to lap up a few much-needed scoops of fresh water. Jack's knees were plastered in mud and his favourite jumper was covered in dog hairs.

Luckily the raft hadn't moved. Adam reached to lift it back onto the bank, still recovering from the shock.

"What was that in his hand? It looked disgusting. Was it a dead animal?" he asked.

"I think it was a rabbit. Maybe he's a hunter or something," replied Jack.

"He sounded German. I recognise the sound of the words from that German boy who was in our class," whispered Adam.

"Yes, you could be right. I didn't think anybody lived down here in these woods. Maybe we should follow him for a little while just to see where he is going," said Jack quietly.

"We should get back to the house. We've been gone now for at least an hour and Jasmine has probably been wondering where we are," replied Adam sensibly.

"But look!" Jack pointed. "That man is heading for a gap in the fence ahead. This is our uncle's land. We should see where exactly he is going. Dad would want us to check it all out!" he said forcefully.

Adam was not too sure what to do. On the one hand, he had had a frightening few moments, but on the other hand, the adrenaline was still pumping through his veins and he did not want this rush to end.

"Okay, we will just find out where he is going and then head back home. If he sees us we'll leg it back to where we came over the electric fence!" Adam said. "I'll keep Club nearby so she doesn't go wandering off," he added.

Jack nodded in agreement, picking up a sturdy-looking dead stick for security.

After hiding the raft under some loose branches, the two boys went up the path where they had seen the man cross over. Sure enough, they spotted him staggering through a large field of uncut grass, the flies still irritating him to judge by the way he waved his stick in the air.

"This really is strange!" said Adam. "I never even knew this field was here before."

Jack and Adam helped Club through the gap in the fence and they both crept carefully behind the man, trying to keep out of sight, ducking behind various trees and plants.

"Good job we wore our wellies!" said Adam as he narrowly avoided a swampy area.

The man had left a clear trail of flattened grass for the boys to follow. Unknowingly he led the boys towards the summit of a hill upon which they saw a small white cottage. The house looked rather run down and was covered in moss.

"Does he live here?" asked Adam. He threw a puzzled look at his brother.

"This is all new to me," Jack replied.

Even Club had a puzzled look on her face. She was sussing out this unusual environment.

"That's far enough!" Adam called out. "I have my binoculars in my pocket so we can try and focus in from here," he said, crouching down on his hunkers.

"What can you see?" asked Jack, wishing he had a pair of binoculars of his own.

A frown gradually grew on Adam's face. As he focused the two large lenses he noticed something dumbfounding in the distance. There was a circle of steel cages to the side of the cottage. There seemed to be creatures moving inside them. The place looked run down, not somewhere you would find trees, never mind a human. He pulled the binoculars away from his eyes and stood back for a moment, wondering if he was seeing things.

"What is it?" asked Jack in an impatient tone.

Adam handed the binoculars to his brother without uttering a word. Jack focused the lenses and lined them up with the house. Sure enough, he also could see steel cages with long bars towards the front. There definitely appeared to be movement within them. It looked like there were dogs of all sizes trapped in these cages. Jack had better eyesight than his older brother and knew about dog breeds, so he could identify border collies, pit bulls and some red setters. Weary moaning sounds echoed from the cages. Jack broke out in a cold sweat of fear. He was normally unfazed by most unpleasant things in life.

"There's dogs inside those cages, that man has them all locked up!" he stuttered.

Adam pulled himself up on his feet.

"Come on Jack, that's enough! We'd better head back and tell someone about this!" he said.

Chapter 5 – Club's Adventure

"Where's Club?" said Adam, looking around frantically.

Jack sprang up and pointed ahead.

"Look, she's over there!" he shrieked, realising that Club had wandered off when they weren't keeping an eye on her. She sniffed her way towards the cottage, ignorant of the surrounding danger.

"If that man sees her he will lock her up in one of those cages like the other dogs!" exclaimed Adam, feeling weak at the knees.

"Club! Club! Come on, girl! Come back!" Jack called.

But Club had another agenda on her mind. She had caught the scent of the other dogs in the distance and was determined to follow it.

Jack and Adam had to act fast. They darted across the long grass, through the dandelions, and knelt down beside the cottage wall across from the circle of cages.

The first thing that caught Adam's attention was the smell. It was horrific. It smelled like the raw meat Mum sometimes had to throw out after it had passed its sell-by date. There was no breeze, which intensified the odour. Jack whistled to get Club's attention but it was no good. He coughed, breathing in a gulp of the toxic air.

The boys began to panic when they heard a door open in the house.

"Oh no! He's coming out,"hissed Jack.

The man stepped out on to the dirt and mud on his front step and threw his hands up the air as he yawned.

"Keep low!" Adam signalled to Jack. They both hunkered down, praying the man would not advance in their direction.

Then the man caught sight of Club, who was now over beside one of the cages, wagging her tail, unaware of what was going on. He murmured something under his breath and bit his lower lip.

He looked in astonishment at this well-fed, healthy-looking Labrador. The man's eyes bulged with vicious intent. He quickly moved around to the other side of the cottage in search of something.

Adam crept along the wall, eager to see where he was going. He saw the man reach inside a yellow pick-up truck parked nearby. The truck had large black tyres that appeared to be stuck in the damp ground. The windows were half open and flies swarmed noisily in and out. He reached inside and pulled out a long pole with a loop of wire at the end of it. Adam didn't like the look of this. The man then turned around and crept towards Club.

Club was usually a friendly dog, but if there was ever a time to get ferocious and fight back, it was now. As she turned around, the man dropped the wire loop around the dog's neck, and pulled. Club moaned in frustration as she tried to escape from the trap. Adam and Jack stared in distress as they watched their favourite pet forced into an open steel cage. The door shut, and their mouths dropped open in horror. The man wore a nasty smirk on his face as he walked back into the old cottage once again.

"We have to do something!" said Adam. He tried to sound confident, but really he was beside himself with worry.

"We should go back and get help," answered Jack, sounding mature in his advice for once.

"You're right, Jack. But we can't leave Club here in case the man does something bad to her," replied Adam. "He could be back out any second. We'll have to try and get her out of that cage before he comes out!"

Adam leaned forward, clutching the stonework of the wall. He focused his binoculars again to see if the man had put a lock on the cage. Luckily it was just bolted across with a thin metal bar. As with their mission to steal biscuits from their Granny's house, the boys knew they had to work as a team to try and rescue Club.

"I'll go for it!" said Jack, taking a deep breath to settle his nerves. "You keep an eye out for me and shout if the man comes out again!"

Jack bent his back to stay low, and ran over to the circle of cages.

All kinds of dogs stared out from behind the steel bars. They looked drowsy. It was almost as if they had no energy to bark out loud.

Jack felt a surge of anger inside him; he could not believe that the man was treating the poor innocent animals like this.

He glanced back at Adam to make sure the coast was clear and then placed his hands on the cold metal bolt on Club's cage. He attempted to slide the bolt, but realised it was going to be more difficult than he had presumed. He used his thumb and index finger to push the bar from left to right.

But it wouldn't budge.

The more he tried, the sweatier his hands became, stopping him from getting a firm grip. He noticed a rag on the ground. He grabbed it and placed it over the bar. He gritted his teeth and heaved the bar from its slot.

Club looked happy to see Jack's face and licked his fingers as the cage door opened. Then she jumped on Jack, licking him up and down as if to say thanks.

Keeping watchful, Jack left the cage unbolted and headed back to where Adam was still crouched down behind the filthy wall.

"Let's get out of here!" Jack cried, and he and Adam ran like they had never run before. The boys wanted to free all of the other animals but they knew it was far too dangerous to wait around any longer.

Forgetting completely about the raft, they flung themselves through the gap back to the woods and scampered down the path with Club close by until they reached the electric fence. They climbed over it and did not stop running until they arrived back in the familiar field beside their house. Jack ran straight by the bullock without even realising it was there. Their wellingtons and socks were covered in dirt and the smell of the man's property seemed to have seeped into the rest of their clothes.

The sun was lower in the sky now, and both boys knew they would have a lot of explaining to do when they arrived back at the house.

Chapter 6 – Jasmine's Relief

Jasmine was out in the garden on her mobile phone and seemed to be in a state of panic. She paced up and down the lawn, looking worried. Adam spotted Diamond sprawled on top of the garden chair. She had presumably been relaxing the whole time.

"Jasmine! Jasmine, we're here!" the boys called out in unison.

Jasmine instantly turned her head and the phone fell from her grasp.

"Where were you two?" she yelled in a relieved voice. She looked angry, to say the least. "I've been looking for you for hours!" she screamed as she forced Club's filthy paws off her black T-shirt.

"We're very sorry," said Adam, bowing his head.

"We can explain what happened!" cried Jack, still panting after his sprint back.

The boys followed Jasmine into the house and began to tell her about their adventure.

When Dad arrived home, the boys could see he was very disappointed that his sons had disobeyed him, and he did not believe them when they told him of what had happened in the woods.

"Nobody lives down there," he said sternly. "And I told you to wait until we all went down together. This was very bold of you two!" His anger made the veins stand out on his forehead.

Both Jack and Adam felt very guilty about letting their Dad down, and realised they could have put themselves in a lot of danger by venturing into the woods without telling anyone.

"But there was a man down there – and the smell, the flies!" Jack blurted out, still full of adrenaline and trying to get his Dad to believe them.

"Calm down, Jack, and talk slower, please," Dad told him, slightly baffled by what he was being told.

"He had dogs captured. He had them locked away in steel cages," Adam said, looking up at his father in the hope that he would give them a chance to explain.

Hearing this from Adam, who was the more sensible of the two, Dad paused.

"We will go down after tea and you boys can show me exactly where you followed this man and where he is supposed to be living," he said in a reluctant voice.

Neither Jack nor Adam wanted to go down to the woods again, but they knew they had to show their Dad what they had discovered.

After a much-needed bite to eat, Dad and the two boys set off down to the woods again, leaving Club behind this time. The three of them plodded down through the tall flowers to the gap where they had followed the strange man up to the hill.

Sure enough, the cages were still there, but to the brothers' astonishment, no dogs were inside. Dad looked stunned when he saw there was a cottage, as the boys had said, and by the look he wore on his face, they knew that he too was beginning to get curious about the whole area. It didn't feel like they were just down the fields, a short distance from home. It felt like a different country.

Dad cautiously walked over to the old mossy door and gave it three firm knocks. The boys had a horrible feeling inside their stomachs. For Adam it was far worse than the anxiety of going back to school. Jack and Adam stood close by their Dad and anxiously awaited any movement in the door.

Dad knocked again, but nobody answered.

"There doesn't seem to be anyone living here," he said warily as he gazed around, taken aback by the toxic fumes.

Adam crept alongside the window sill and tried to look inside, but his view was blocked by the dirt and grime on the inner pane of the window. He looked back towards Jack in a state of confusion. Where had this man gone? And where were all the dogs? They gave each other a questioning look.

It was a mystery.

Then Adam remembered that he had seen the yellow pick-up truck earlier. He couldn't see it now. He walked over to where it had been and saw fresh skid marks on the muddy ground, with a track leading out to another section of the woods.

"He must have fled out this way, with the cages in the back," said Adam, trying his best to connect some of the dots.

As they moved around the cottage, they all saw things they would have preferred not to have seen. There were some remains of small woodland creatures like squirrels, rabbits and hares, tossed down beside the flowers. They were infested with maggots and creepy crawlies. Beside them were more steel traps and a variety of glass jars thrown about in the grass.

Adam looked at his father. Dad's face had turned white and he was shaking his head in bewilderment.

The three hurried back towards the path with butterflies in their stomachs and set off to pull the raft out from where it had been left. The excitement surrounding it had gone. They were supposed to be looking forward to trying it out on the stream, but now all Jack and Adam could think about was the horrible man they had encountered earlier.

Dad led the way back to the house along the usual route. They talked to each other all the way about the whole scenario and wondered what would be the best way of finding out more.

"Maybe we should ring George," said Jack, knowing well that this would create some form of drama over the next couple of days.

George was Dad's brother, a farmer who had grown up on the land. Adam and Jack knew that George would never allow anyone to pull the wool over his eyes and would want to know what was going on in the area.

"I think you are right, Jack," replied Dad, flicking away some of the midges that were annoying him.

Mum was extremely disappointed at her sons' disobedience, and seemed just as confused as the others, but within twenty minutes of arriving back at the house Dad had rung George to tell him the story. The boys could see by the reaction on their father's face that George too was shocked at the news.

"Well, maybe you are right, George!" Dad said finally, ending the telephone conversation.

Jack and Adam gathered around their father, eagerly awaiting the next plan of attack. He told them that George was going to call the police to look into the matter. At first the boys thought that this measure might be a little extreme, but George felt very strongly about finding out exactly who had been trespassing down in this area of the woods.

When two male police officers arrived the next day, the boys and their father, accompanied by George, escorted them towards the entrance to the field and set off down to the woods once again. Club was in great form, loving every minute of the commotion and the gathering of people. She also had the chance to get a sniff of George, whom she had only seen through the gates before. They all headed off with the sun beaming down on the two boys' backs.

When they arrived on the scene, the police appeared perplexed – just as the boys and their father had been. Dad outlined what he had discovered and directed the police officers' attention towards the animal carcasses and traps before moving towards the tyre marks left behind by the pick-up truck.

The smell was still disgusting and each person covered his mouth with his hand. Club had to be held back, as she had picked up the scent of raw meat and would have started chewing at some of the animal bones if given the chance.

After carefully photographing the scene outside, the policeman in charge advanced to the door and knocked several times. There were only echoes to be heard. Then they barged the door in. The policemen stepped inside, but everyone else was advised to stay back and wait outside.

But Jack and Adam just had to have a look.

The boys scampered around to a side window and Jack boosted Adam up onto the window ledge. This window wasn't covered in as much dirt and grime so Adam could see the officers rooting about inside.

The room looked dark and damp. He could see more cages of various sizes inside. He saw long sharp things on the ground like needles, with very long tips, just lying on the bare floor. The police were using gloves to place several of these needles into their plastic bags. Adam moved his head up and down to get a view of the different parts of the room. He couldn't understand how anyone could be living there. There were no signs of furniture or any areas for storing food. It was all very eerie.

Jack, Dad and George looked in at the door as the policemen continued to pick up more strange items and place them in their forensic bags. George seemed impatient. It looked like he couldn't handle the suspense anymore, and pushed through the door to see what was going on.

Adam saw George enter the room. He stared as if he had just witnessed a death. He was no sooner inside than he wanted to come back out.

"What's in there, Adam?" asked Jack, jumping up and down trying to catch a glimpse inside.

"This guy must have left in a hurry. Everything looks like it has been cleared out," answered Adam. He jumped back down from the window ledge and went round to meet the officers as they left the cottage.

"We'll go back to the station and send some of these needles and swabs off to the lab for fingerprints and further examination," one of the policemen explained. He reached to pick up more items, and dropped them into a plastic zip-lock bag.

"What do you think is going on?" George inquired, staring one of the policemen in the eyes.

"We honestly don't know, sir, but we will do our best to get the facts," the officer responded. He closed the door behind him and stretched out some red tape to cordon off the property.

"It appears like someone was here alright, and something strange, to say the least, was taking place. We will report back and send out a forensic team to have a closer look tomorrow," the other officer concluded.

Chapter 7 –On the Run!

When the police had left Jack and Adam headed straight up the treehouse steps to try and make sense of the new revelations. Even though it was quite late the sun was still setting and some light made its way through the two small windows.

"You should have seen George's face when he entered the cottage. It must have been awful in there," said Adam, scratching his head.

"I know, and with all that red tape around the property now, it's like a big murder investigation," replied Jack.

"Luckily our Club wasn't murdered. Who knows what he would have done to you?" Adam said, bending down to cuddle the dog. As he did so, something attached to Club's right leg caught his eye.

He lifted the leg. Stuck to Club's fur was a piece of yellow paper. It was a sticky note, covered in fur and crinkled up.

"What's this?" said Adam. He lifted the paper up gently and opened it out. On the paper was a list of numbers. They were written clearly and there was just enough light to make them out.

Jack moved in for a closer look. "That looks like a phone number, Adam. Where do you think it came from?" he asked.

"I bet it stuck to Club earlier when she was in the cage. It might be his number," suggested Adam. "What should we do?"

Jack took the piece of paper and counted the numbers.

"That's definitely a phone number. I bet it's a number the woodsman rang – maybe one of his contacts. Wait there!" said Jack.

Club looked on as Jack sped down the stairs and up the lawn. Adam watched out of the window, wondering what he was up to. Minutes later Jack was back at base, panting heavily. Then he showed Adam Dad's mobile phone.

"Adam, I know you won't like this, but trust me I know what I'm doing," said Jack, still out of breath.

"You can't be doing what I think you're doing," said Adam.

"Listen, all we need to do is be smart about this and we'll get some evidence to help the police. Just go with me!" Jack unlocked the phone and typed out a message. Adam just stared.

I'm using a new number, I need some more stuff, meet me at the cottage ASAP

Jack then entered the number on the sticky note and crossed his fingers for a quick reply.

"You think this number might belong to one of the man's contacts?" asked Adam with a croak in his voice.

"It's worth a shot. Did you see all of those needles the police found earlier? This number could lead us to the person who is supplying him with all of this, you never know," answered Jack, putting the phone down on top of a stool.

The two brothers waited and waited, staring at the setting sun, well aware that at any minute their parents would be calling for them to come in for the night.

"This new number thing is suspicious. What if the person rings us? What do we do then?" asked Adam, starting to feel unwell.

No sooner had he spoken than there was a beep from Dad's phone. Jack grabbed it, his heart racing. It was a message. It was from the number on the yellow paper.

The message read: *OK*.

"This is it. Adam. Come on, we have to go down again."

"We'll get Dad," said Adam, feeling himself coming out in a cold sweat.

"We don't have time. Come on!" hissed Jack, pulling his brother by the T-shirt. He dragged his brother down to the back of the shed, ready to jump over the wall and race down the field again.

Adam looked over his shoulder to see if his Mum or Dad were watching out the window. He knew he and his brother were doing wrong again, but there were so many emotions running through his head he couldn't think properly.

He raced with Jack all the way down to where the police had cordoned off the area. It was very dark and creepy in the woods and the boys were glad when they arrived in the open area where the cottage lay.

Jack pulled out his Dad's phone and activated the camera mode. Neither of the boys smelt the horrible odour that still lingered. All they were thinking about was getting this person on camera and then getting safely back to their house.

"We'll have to go up this tree, it's the only way to get some good footage," whispered Jack, conscious that time was ticking and the person could arrive at any minute.

"There's no point the two of us going up. I'm hiding here. Make sure you don't fall," said Adam.

He watched as his brother held the phone in one hand and raised his other arm to lift himself up onto the first branch. Adam nestled back in the bushes with a good view of anyone coming from the gap. The sounds of insects made him want to scratch all the time. He felt as if they were crawling all over him.

Just then a thought crossed his mind. What about the other track that the woodsman had left by when fleeing the scene in his pick-up truck? What if the person on the end of the phone came in that way? They wouldn't be able to see the person at all. He knew all he and his brother could do was wait and hope for the best. Jack was now up as far as he needed to be and was leaning on a thick branch at the top. He had the camera on the phone all ready to record. He concentrated on breathing in and out to settle his nerves.

Suddenly Adam held his breath. He could hear the sound of feet walking through the grass. Peering out from his hiding place he could see something white making its way towards them. As it got closer, Adam could make out the shape of a small man wearing a long white cloak. He looked like a person who worked in a laboratory of some kind.

Jack was keeping as still as he could while holding the camera out to capture everything he could see. He was conscious of the fact that the camera generated a bright light so he tried his best to hold it still and not draw attention. Jack could see the man was holding a brown box in his left hand.

As the man came closer to the cottage he raised his head and came to an abrupt stop. He gazed around, noticing all the red tape that now surrounded the area. Adam could see that the man knew something was up.

Then the man reached for his phone and began pressing some buttons. Straight away Adam realised something. He was about to ring Dad's phone. He looked up to see if Jack had noticed. Jack had, and was doing his best to turn the phone off.

Ring, ring! went the phone before Jack could switch it off.

The man looked up warily through the trees to where the sound was coming from.

Adam feared for his brother's safety. He grabbed a few stones and threw them in the opposite direction. The man turned around sharply when he heard the stones clatter against some timber. Then he turned his head back to the trees, paused for a moment, and ran off the way he had come, towards the woods.

When all was silent again Adam popped his head out from the bushes and looked up at his brother. Jack was clinging to the tree in fright, still clutching the mobile in his hand.

"Come on, Jack, we have to go!" ordered Adam. Enough was enough, he thought. This was the second time today they had risked their lives.

Jack made his way stiffly down the tree and set off with Adam through the dark woods and back safely to their house.

Throughout the next day all the boys could think about was what had happened. Luckily Jack had caught some footage of the mysterious little man and both he and Adam watched it over and over again when they had a chance to get their Dad's phone. Although the footage was quite blurred, Jack had got a shot of the man's face. He had small eyes and sallow skin, as if he rarely went out in daylight.

At eight o'clock that evening a squad car arrived at the door. Mum immediately imagined the worst and looked out into the back garden to make sure the boys were safe. Thankfully she could see Jack pulling a white blanket over Diamond, who tossed it off her head.

She opened the door to see a man and a woman standing there. They were both dressed very professionally in sharp suits. The man was quite tall and wore sunglasses. He produced an identification badge and then introduced himself and his female colleague as detectives, explaining they had been assigned to exploring further the suspicious matter in the woods.

"What did you find out?" Dad asked them as they stepped into the house.

"Well, we have some news alright," announced the man, removing his sunglasses.

Adam and Jack raced inside. The man, with his combed hair and sunglasses in hand, reminded them of a character from a *Larry Right* episode.

"What sort of news?" Mum asked. "Was there someone living down there?"

"Yes indeed there was!" the man said. He looked anxiously towards his partner. "It turns out that a man named Fredrick Potter has been living – or at least locating himself – down in these woods for the last number of months."

"Fredrick who? Who is this guy?" Dad asked.

"This man has been wanted by the FBI for the last year and a half. He is a fugitive on the run," he added.

Jack's eyes lit up a little with a mixture of excitement and anxiety.

"What for?" asked Dad curiously.

"He is an Austrian-born scientist who has a record of organising dog fights between different breeds," said the woman. She was small and had sharp features but soft eyes. "People gamble on the outcome of the fights. Only one dog survives. Potter is notorious. He has developed a chemical that can transform any tame, good-natured dog into a savage killer." Everyone stood open-mouthed.

"We had an inkling this whole scenario looked like some of Potter's previous schemes," the woman went on. "So we got our whole team to make this investigation a priority."

"Oh my God, that's awful! Where is this guy now? Did you find him?" Mum asked, breathing more and more heavily all the time.

"This guy is a bit of a ghost. He comes and goes but people never seem able to pinpoint him. He always appears to choose a woodland location for his work, but we have no clue where he will go next. The search is on-going," added the woman.

"However, Mr Potter did slip up this time," said the man. "He normally leaves no evidence where he has been. This time he seems to have left in a rush, forgetting to clean up some of his mess. He left behind a small notebook in which several names of chemists and doctors were written. We intend to use these names to find and capture him. When we find him we have enough evidence to send him to jail for a long time!" he said, pleased about this at least.

"He must have realised that someone let Club out of the cage, and raced off for fear of being caught," said Jack quietly to his brother.

"Yeah, and that little guy must have been his one of his contacts," responded Adam.

Jack nodded as he pieced this information together in his head.

"You two boys were very lucky this man did not spot you. He has a record of being very dangerous, and not just to dogs!" said the woman, eyeing up Jack in particular as if she knew he was a troublemaker.

Jack understood what the detective was trying to tell him. He had seen Fredrick's eyes. They were eyes that were disturbed and menacing.

"Thank God we released Club before she disappeared too!" said Adam, frowning at Jack.

The detectives went on to explain that teams

were currently down in the woods looking for the man.

"Did you find any of the dogs that were captured?" asked Jack.

"Yes, some of the captured dogs were located. However, they were injured and visibly shaken from what they had to endure," replied the man.

"You'd better take a look at this as well," said Jack. He plucked up the courage to move forward and handed the man Dad's phone, along with the little yellow note with the number on it. "We did some investigating of our own."

Their parents stood open-mouthed as the detective pressed *Play*. Then they all huddled round the phone to watch the video.

Jack nodded at Adam to tell his brother to follow him down the hall before Mum and Dad began asking awkward questions.

As the boys walked back to the kitchen, all sorts of emotions tossed around in their heads and stomachs. What a couple of days it had been! Their minds wandered back overall the little things they had witnessed in their adventure. They both wondered where exactly this Fredrick Potter was now and whether he had other plans to set down in other secluded woods, and other experiments to carry out.

The brothers looked at each other and breathed out with relief.

"He's still out there. What if we meet him again? I wonder who those names are in the notebook, and could they be more fugitives?" asked Adam fearfully. "Maybe that yellow piece of paper with the number fell from that notebook too," he added.

Jack shook his head. He didn't have any answers, but hated the thought of someone getting away with harming innocent animals, especially dogs. After several minutes of thinking, his eyes lit up with an idea.

"Maybe dogs can be used against him!" he said, then paused for a few seconds in thought.

"Eh? What do you mean?" asked Adam, more puzzled than ever.

"Well, this Potter guy had spent most of his life capturing dogs and experimenting with them, right? What if dogs can be used to capture him?

Dogs would just need his scent." He reached for a cool glass of water from the kitchen tap. "I picked up a rag that was down next to the cages when I was trying to open the steel bolt. I think I left it in the treehouse. That has to have his scent on it!" he added excitedly.

"Follow me – I have a plan!" he said, a cunning smile on his lips.

Before Adam could make eye contact, his brother was already out the door. As he stepped out onto his back yard, heading towards the treehouse, he signalled for Club to join him, wondering what scheme Jack was about to concoct this time.

The End

Books in *'The Adventures of Jack and Adam'* series

For more information on 'The Adventures of
Jack and Adam' series, please visit us on
www.jackandadamadventures.com

Also by Anthony Broderick
'The Larry Right' Series

eBooks now available in the Larry Right series

For more information, please visit us on
www.jackandadamadventures.com